BIONICLE
MASK OF LIGHT

by C.A. Hapka

SCHOLASTIC INC.
New York Toronto London Auckland Sydney
Mexico City New Delhi Hong Kong Buenos Aires

ISBN 0-439-50118-0

© 2003 The LEGO Group. LEGO, the LEGO logo, BIONICLE,
and the BIONICLE logo are registered trademarks of The LEGO Group
and are used here by special permission.
All rights reserved. Published by Scholastic Inc.
SCHOLASTIC and associated logos are trademarks and/or
registered trademarks of Scholastic Inc.

12 11 10 9 8 7 6   4 5 6 7 8/0

Printed in the U.S.A.
First printing, September 2003

THE MYSTERY MASK

"Takua?" Jaller called urgently. "Takua?"

There was no answer. Jaller grumbled under his breath, then hurried toward the Wall of History, a stone carving that decorated one side of the village of Ta-Koro. The wall was covered with the brave deeds of the great hero Toa Tahu, who had been foretold through legends long before he and the other five Toa had ever appeared on the lush tropical island of Mata Nui.

Jaller reached the Wall of History. He saw Takua's kolhii stick leaning against it. Kolhii was the island's most popular sport, and Takua and Jaller were *supposed* to be on their way to a match.

"Takua!" Jaller shouted, annoyed. He hurried through the door carved into the wall.

1

Jaller raced down the steps. At the bottom he found himself in a lava runoff tunnel. Ahead, he could hear a deep rumble, which grew louder and louder as he walked on.

Finally the tunnel widened into a cave. A wide river of lava flowed through it, tumbling relentlessly toward a steep drop-off — the spectacular thousand-foot Lava Falls.

But Jaller paid no attention to the falls. He had just spotted a small figure hopping from rock to rock across the lava flow. The figure was wearing a blue mask and carrying a lava board under one arm. On the shore at the edge of the cave, a crablike Ussal was waiting patiently. Jaller recognized her as Takua's faithful pet, Pewku.

"Takua!" Jaller yelled. "What are you doing down here?"

Takua winced. He'd forgotten all about the kolhii game.

"Oh, yeah," he said. "Sorry, Jaller. Hang on a sec, I just want to check out that totem." He pointed to a stone pillar just ahead.

Jaller glanced toward it. "You're hopping across *lava* to look at a stupid warning totem?"

"I got curious." Takua grinned.

Jaller sighed. "Do you know what Turaga Vakama would say?"

Takua shrugged. "Can't say exactly," he said lightly. "But I'm betting the word *irresponsible* would come up."

Takua hopped to the next rock, trying not to think about what Vakama, the leader of the village, would say or do if he found out about this.

Now that he was here, Takua wasn't about to turn back before reaching his goal.

Soon he was only one jump away from the edge of the island. It was a long jump, but he didn't hesitate. He flung himself toward the shore. His hands scrabbled for a hold as one foot slipped back toward the lava. He felt the sizzle of heat and yanked his foot to safety. Leaping to his feet, he grinned and bowed.

Jaller couldn't help smiling. "Very impressive," he said. "Now let's go!"

Takua barely heard him. Now that he was closer, the totem sign on the stone pillar looked stranger and more interesting than ever. He pulled it loose and turned it over in his hands.

"Huh," Takua murmured as he stared at the symbol inscribed upon the stone. It was like nothing he'd ever seen before.

Suddenly there was a rumble, loud enough to overcome the distant roar of the falls. Takua glanced up just in time to see the stone pillar beside him sink into the ground. The island and its surroundings began to quake violently.

"Whaa — *oof*!" Takua cried as the sudden quake knocked him off his feet. The totem slipped from his grasp. Takua lunged for it, but he was too late. The totem slipped into the lava and disappeared. "Aah," Takua groaned in disappointment.

"Hurry up!" Jaller called, as the cavern's stone ceiling began to crumble under the force of the quake.

A section of the wall cracked and collapsed. Lava spurted through the opening, swelling the river within the cavern. Takua gulped as the rising river wiped out the path of stones he'd used to reach the island. How was he supposed to get back to shore now?

Before he could figure that out, he was nearly blinded by a sudden beam of brilliant light. *What in the name of Mata Nui is that?* he wondered, squinting toward the source of the light.

It was a mask. A mask like the ones he and Jaller and every other Matoran wore — but different. This mask glowed with the light of a thousand suns. It was floating in the lava, unharmed by the intense heat.

Only a Toa's mask can do something like that, Takua thought in awe.

"Jaller!" he called. "Look!"

Jaller's eyes widened as the mask floated past the spot where he and Pewku were standing. "A Great Kanohi mask!"

Takua leaned out over the edge of the island. He had to get that mask!

The Kanohi mask danced and whirled just out of reach. If he could just stretch a little farther . . .

Got it! he thought with triumph as he finally grabbed the edge of the mask. Pushing himself back from the edge of the river, he sat and studied his prize, which seemed to glow more brightly than ever. He was barely aware that the quake was fading away as quickly as it had come. He turned over the mask to reveal strange, incomprehensible writing on the other side.

"Wow," he murmured curiously. "Never seen this language . . ."

"Takua!" Jaller called.

Takua had almost forgotten about his friend. Glancing up, he recognized the look of impatience on Jaller's face. He climbed to his feet, still holding the mask.

"Hold your Rahi, I'm coming," he called back.

"Oh, really?" Jaller replied. "Learned to fly, have you?"

Takua grimaced, remembering that his path

of stones was now under the lava. He was stranded. Or was he? "Here," he called to his friend. "Take the mask." Without waiting for an answer, he heaved the mask across the river.

Jaller caught the mask. *Hmmm,* he thought. *It looked much brighter from a distance. Must have been a reflection from the lava. . . .*

As he looked up again, he saw Takua holding up his lava board and suddenly realized what his friend was planning to do. He gulped.

"Are you sure about this?" Jaller called nervously.

"Not at all!" Takua replied cheerfully. He grabbed a flat, paddle-shaped stone. Then he took a deep breath and flung his lava board forward. "AAAAAAAAAAAAAAAH!" he cried.

As the board landed in the lava at the river's edge, he leaped onto it. The motion sent him skimming forward over the bubbling lava. But he soon started to lose momentum. The current tugged at the board, turning it toward the falls.

Uh-oh, Takua thought. Using the flat stone

he was holding, he started to paddle. He kept his gaze on Jaller and Pewku, who were watching anxiously from the shore.

Suddenly there was a new rumble. The cavern wall collapsed into the river with a splash, freeing a torrent of lava from behind it. The lava burst forward in a huge wave, rushing down the river toward the helpless Takua.

Jaller froze in horror. There was no time to shout a warning — and no time for Takua to get away.

RIDING THE WAVE

Takua stared at the wave rushing toward him, mesmerized by its size and power. Suddenly a huge red figure appeared at the far side of the river, blending in with the fiery color of the lava. He surfed across the river, impossibly fast, heading directly toward Takua as the wave crested.

A moment later, Takua felt himself grabbed and yanked out of the path of the wave.

"Toa Tahu!" he exclaimed in surprise.

Tahu flung Takua onto his back.

"Chronicler!" Tahu said over his shoulder as he surfed expertly across the lava. "Sight-seeing, were you? Let's take a closer look at those falls."

Back on the shore, Jaller saw the huge figure of the Toa of Fire suddenly emerge from in front of the lava wave.

He watched as the Toa shot straight off the edge of the falls and disappeared. A split second later the wave of lava crashed down, spurting over the falls.

Jaller shuddered with horror, feeling his knees go weak. Takua! There was no way he could have escaped the lava. *Toa Tahu was too late*, he thought bleakly.

Meanwhile, Tahu surfed down the sheer vertical face of Lava Falls.

Takua clung to the Toa's shoulders, hardly daring to keep his eyes open. Tahu's skill had carried them this far — but how was he going to save them from plunging into the lava at the base of the falls?

Then he made the mistake of glancing up. He gulped in terror as he saw the enormous lava wave rushing toward them.

Their fall suddenly stopped short. Scrambling to keep hold of Tahu's shoulders, he saw that the Toa had broken his lava board into two pieces — twin magma swords. He had plunged those swords into the solid rock behind the falls.

"So, Takua," the Toa said teasingly. "Is this view close enough?"

Takua was too petrified to speak. Finally he found his voice again. "*Incoming!*"

Tahu glanced up at the lava wave, which was nearly upon them. A translucent red force field shot out from his mask, surrounding him and Takua in a glowing sphere of energy.

The lava wave thundered over and around them, but the red force field protected them from its touch.

As the shielding force field faded, Tahu pulled one of his swords out of the rock. He reached up and stabbed it back in a little higher, pulling himself and Takua up the cliff like an ice climber. Takua held on as the Toa climbed steadily upward, one sword's length at a time, trying to calm the wild, terrified beating of his heart.

At the top of the falls, Jaller was kneeling in grief beside a sobbing Pewku. *Why did he have to do it?* he wondered. *Was this stupid mask really worth it? We could all be safe at the kolhii tournament right now. . . .*

His grief was interrupted by Toa Tahu somersaulting into view from over the edge of the
falls. Jaller jumped in surprise.

"Toa Tahu!" he cried with a sudden burst
of hope. But there was no sign of Takua at the
Toa's side, and Jaller quickly slumped into sadness
again. "Takua?" he asked quietly. "He didn't . . ."

Suddenly Takua hopped to the ground
from somewhere behind the Toa's back. He was
grinning from ear to ear. Pewku jumped toward
her master happily, nearly knocking him over.

Jaller leaped to his feet as well, flooded
with relief. "You're alive!" he cried. "Kolhii-head!
You could've been lava bones!"

"Could've been," Takua said, gently pushing
away the enthusiastic Pewku. "But I'm not."

Tahu was staring at the mask in Jaller's
hands. He reached over and grabbed it.

"A Great Kanohi mask," he said in surprise.

"It was in the lava," Jaller told the Toa.
"Takua —"

"This could be important," Tahu interrupted, handing the mask back to Jaller. "Take it to Turaga Vakama."

Jaller nodded and turned away, ready to do what the suddenly stern Toa had ordered. But Tahu stopped him with a smile.

"*After* you've won the kolhii match," Tahu finished. "Now get going, and no sight-seeing!"

"Yes, Toa Tahu!" Jaller said happily. He raced toward the steps back up to the village, with Takua and Pewku right behind him.

THE MIGHTY TOA

"Today is a great day for our village of Ta-Koro," Turaga Vakama proclaimed. His gaze wandered over the crowded stadium. Villagers from three of the six villages of Mata Nui were crowded into the carved stone bleachers. One section of the bleachers overflowed with a rowdy, brown-masked group from the desert village of Po-Koro, while the quieter, more thoughtful residents of the watery village of Ga-Koro watched with amusement. The hosting Ta-Matoran were scattered throughout the crowd.

Three of the six Toa Nuva sat on a special dais overlooking the scene. The Turaga smiled and bowed slightly toward them.

"We are thankful to the Great Spirit for his

gift of six guardians who represent the elements," he continued. "Fire. Water. Earth. Air. Ice. And Stone. Our mighty Toa, whose valiant quests and heroic deeds have saved us many times from the forces of Makuta . . ."

There was a visible shudder from the crowd as the Turaga spoke the name of the island's dark, mysterious enemy.

". . . and given us hope for the future, for our history's next chapter."

Turaga Vakama bowed to the Toa. "Three of these protectors are with us today. Let us welcome them," he announced. "First, the spirit of Fire, Toa Tahu!"

As the Turaga spoke his name, Tahu stood and leaped onto the wall behind the Toa's box. He waved his magma swords, sending a ribbon of fire searing through the air.

The crowd roared with delight.

"From the village of water," Vakama proclaimed, "Toa Gali! And from the village of stone, Toa Pohatu!"

Gali stood, raising her blue-handled aqua

ax in salute to the cheering crowd. Nearby, Pohatu did the same, giving a friendly wave with his bronze-tinged climbing claws.

Vakama continued, praising all the Toa for their brave deeds. As he spoke, Tahu turned and bowed to Gali, who was still standing. "Pleasure to see you again, Gali," he said.

"Thank you, Tahu."

The Fire Toa gestured to the seat beside his own. But Gali sat down in a different seat, leaving an empty one between the two of them.

Rolling his eyes, Pohatu leaped over Tahu and sat down between them. He put a friendly arm over the shoulders of each of them.

"You two," he said with a shake of his head. "Still so ill at ease?"

Gali raised one eyebrow playfully. "I think my brother is afraid of having his fire extin- guished," she said, glancing past Pohatu at Tahu.

"Sister," Tahu responded, his own tone just as light and playful, "against me you'd be nothing but steam — hot air, as they say."

Below, the Turaga were watching the Toa's exchange. Onewa, the Turaga of Po-Koro, shook his head worriedly. "The Toa squabble like Gukkos over a berry," he remarked.

Turaga Nokama of Ga-Koro nodded. "Their recent victories are a blessing," she said, "but they've forgotten how they need one another."

Turaga Vakama had paused in his speech just long enough to hear them. "Indeed, Nokama," he said, glancing up at the Toa with concern.

Then he stepped forward once again. He raised his arm, and the crowd quieted.

"We dedicate this new kolhii field to the Great Spirit, Mata Nui," Vakama said. "And to the three virtues: unity, duty, destiny."

"Unity, duty, destiny!" the gathered Matoran cried in unison.

Turaga Vakama smiled. "Let the tournament begin!"

WINNER TAKES ALL

"Ta-Koro welcomes three teams!"

Takua shivered with anticipation as the kolhii announcer's voice rolled over the stadium.

A section of the arena wall spun around to reveal a kolhii goal — a large stone carving of the face of the Great Spirit, Mata Nui. Two brown-masked players strode out.

"From the desert village of Po-Koro," the announcer said, "Copper Mask winners and undisputed kolhii champions . . . Hewkii and Hafu!"

The players raised their sticks in salute, and the crowd cheered wildly.

Another section of the wall spun and revealed another goal. This time a pair of blue-masked players stepped out onto the field.

"From Ga-Koro, the challengers — Hahli and Macku!" the announcer cried.

As the crowd cheered, Takua gripped his kolhii stick tighter. They were next.

The third and final goal spun into view, and Takua bounded onto the field with his friend and teammate beside him.

"And from Ta-Koro, the Captain of the Guard and the Chronicler, Jaller and Takua!"

Takua waved his kolhii stick at the crowd, enjoying their applause.

"Try your new move," Jaller whispered to him. "The crowd'll go crazy."

Takua shrugged. "Nah," he replied. "It only works in practice."

He raised his stick toward Jaller. Jaller clunked it with his own. Then they parted and took their positions — Jaller in front of the goal, and Takua in the center of the field facing the other offense players.

"Play well," Hewkii said. Hahli and Takua repeated the words.

Then the three of them huddled around the circle in the center of the field. They didn't have long to wait before the circle spun open and a pair of kolhii balls shot out and into the air.

Takua moved instantly, lunging at one of the balls. But Hahli was faster — she scooped up the ball and jumped away. Takua spun toward the second ball. Hewkii was leaping toward it, too — both of them swatted at the ball with their sticks, trying to knock each other aside.

Finally Takua saw the net on the end of his stick swoop the ball out of midair. Yes! He had it!

He spun around . . . a little too fast. His foot hit his own kolhii stick, and he tripped and fell. The ball rolled out and Hewkii jumped forward, kicking it away.

Disgusted with himself, Takua raced after Hewkii. The two of them dodged and weaved, their feet flying as they battled for control of the ball.

Jaller saw Hahli sprinting toward him, pushing the second ball with the hammer end of her stick. She flipped the ball into the air, using the stick to smash it toward the Ta-Koro goal.

Jaller swung his stick — interception!

Hahli smiled and raised her stick to salute Jaller's defense. "Not bad," she said breathlessly.

Jaller crossed his arms and tilted his head. "Nothing gets by the Captain of the Guard," he bragged playfully. He smiled. "Unless he wishes it."

Hahli returned his smile. Then she turned and walked away.

Hewkii had gained control of the other ball. He raced across the field toward the Ga-Koro goal with Takua in hot pursuit.

With a burst of speed, Takua darted past and flung himself on the ground directly in Hewkii's path. Without missing a step, Hewkii vaulted over him. Takua looked sideways just in time to see Hewkii flip the ball into the air and kick it toward the goal. The Ga-Matoran defensive player, Macku, dove for the flying ball, but it sailed past her.

"And Hewkii scores!" the announcer shouted.

It's just one goal, Takua told himself. *There's still plenty of time for us to catch up.*

*   *   *

Some time later, Takua was feeling less optimistic. There were two lightstones on the scoreboard for Po-Koro now, along with two for Ga-Koro. The Ta-Matoran team had yet to score a goal.

Kolhii was played to a winning score of three goals. To catch up, the Ta-Matoran had to sink three goals in a row. Such a thing was almost unheard of in the sport.

Takua clutched his kolhii stick, preparing himself as he waited for the balls to emerge.

When they popped out of the circle, he dove toward them. But Hahli was ready. Ducking low, she quickly swiped her stick back and forth, sending both balls skittering out in different directions.

When the balls hit the ground, Takua leaped toward one. So did Hewkii. The two of them smashed into each other in midair, each falling back with a grunt as the ball went flying upward again.

Both players leaped to their feet and again

dove for the ball. Takua managed to scoop it up just before Hewkii reached it.

Yes! Takua thought, using the stick to vault into the air and over Hewkii's head. As Takua somersaulted in midair, he flung the scoop end of the stick forward, shooting the kolhii ball out of it in a blur.

But the shot was wide — so wide that it sailed right over the top of the Ga-Matoran goal and into the stands. The spectators in that section dove for cover as the ball careened into the seats.

Takua was so busy trying to watch the ball that he didn't pay attention to his own somersault. He hit the ground face-first.

"Ooh!" the announcer said. "I don't think we've seen *that* move before!"

Takua sat up and spit out a mouthful of dust. So much for his special move! *I told Jaller it wouldn't work,* he thought in disgust.

As he looked around, he was just in time to see Hahli sprint past, still kicking the second kolhii ball in front of her. She closed in on the Ta-Matoran goal and whacked the ball with her stick. Jaller dove at it, but it sailed past his out-stretched hand — and straight into the goal.

"Hahli scores!" the announcer cried. "Goal and tournament to Ga-Koro!"

The Ga-Matoran section of the crowd went wild, jumping up and down and cheering loudly for their team.

In the Toa box, Pohatu turned to Gali and offered his fist. She clanked it with her own, grin-ning widely. Then Gali turned and held out her fist to Tahu. Tahu stared down at the ground, not returning the gesture.

Back on the field, Takua dragged himself af-ter Jaller, who was hurrying to join the other players after grabbing his kolhii bag from the sidelines. He couldn't believe they'd lost — and it was all his own fault!

Jaller extended his stick to Hahli. "Not bad," he said with a grin. "For a *Ga-Matoran*."

Hahli tapped his stick with her own, ignor-ing the joke. Then she turned to Takua. "Good ef-

Mask of Light

fort, Takua," she said warmly. "Nice move back there — a little more practice and you'll have something amazing."

"Thanks," he said tonelessly, not bothering to look up. It would be a long time before he got over this. A very long time.

Turaga Vakama stepped forward. "Congratulations to Ga-Koro!" he said. "And well played by all."

The players all turned and raised their sticks in salute to the hosting Turaga. As Jaller raised his stick, the motion jostled the kolhii bag he'd slung over his shoulder. The mysterious Kanohi mask fell out and landed on the ground, rolling against Takua's foot.

The crowd cried out in amazement as a beam of brilliant, clear light shot out of the mask — aiming straight at Jaller.

25

THE HERALD

Jaller staggered backward, briefly blinded by the beam glaring right into his face.

The crowd was murmuring in amazement. Turaga Vakama stepped forward, his eyes filled with awe. "Come," he said, reaching for the mask. "We must take this to the suva immediately."

A few minutes later most of the crowd was gathered around the suva, a small, domelike shrine in the center of the village.

Nokama, the Turaga of Ga-Koro, was chanting under her breath as she stretched her hands toward the floating mask.

"*Mapaku una-kanokee wehnua-hakeeta ah-keelahe hanoni rahun-ahk toa-nak panokeeta makuta-tahkee ohnah-koo,*" she mumbled.

"What's she doing?" Jaller whispered.

"Translating?" Takua guessed.

Finally Nokama reached up and pulled the mask out of the air.

"This is the Great Kanohi Mask of Light," she said solemnly. "A mask to be worn *only* . . . by the Seventh Toa, the Toa of Light."

The onlookers gasped. A Seventh Toa?

Turaga Vakama stepped forward. "Legends foretell the coming of a Seventh Toa, who would bring light to the shadows and awaken Mata Nui."

Tahu leaped down from his perch on the nearby village wall. "What are we waiting for?" he cried. "We should prepare for this Toa's arrival! When will it be? And where?"

Turaga Onewa shook his head. "Ah, this Toa will not simply appear as you and the others did," he said. "The Seventh Toa must be found!"

The crowd murmured in amazement. The original six Toa had not needed finding — they had appeared suddenly on the island just when the Matoran needed them most.

"The Mask of Light chose who would find it," Nokama said. "Perhaps it also chose who would deliver it to its master."

"Wait," Tahu exclaimed. "At the stadium, there was a sign! The mask threw all its light upon one Matoran." He pointed. "Jaller — he must be the Herald of the Seventh Toa!"

"B-but I didn't . . ." Jaller stammered. He turned to Takua. "Tell them the truth!" he whispered urgently. "Say something!"

Takua knew what his friend wanted — to tell the crowd that it had been Takua, not Jaller, who had found the mask. But Takua wasn't about to take responsibility for this. Who knew how he would manage to mess up such an important quest! No, this was a job for someone responsible. Someone mature.

Someone like Jaller.

Takua raised his kolhii stick. "Hail Jaller!" he cried. "Herald of the Seventh Toa! All hail Jaller!"

The crowd joined in with enthusiasm. "HAIL JALLER!"

Vakama pointed his firestaff at Jaller. "Captain of the Guard!" he called. "Approach!"

Jaller had no choice. He started toward the group of Turaga . . . then paused just long enough to grab Takua.

Vakama held the Mask of Light out to Jaller. "It seems the mask has chosen you," he said solemnly. "Will you seek the Seventh Toa?"

Jaller glanced at Takua, who refused to meet his eye. "I — I will," Jaller said. "And Takua has volunteered to join me!"

As the crowd thinned out, the Toa gathered on the wall above the suva. "A Seventh Toa . . ." Tahu said, sounding puzzled. "But why now? All the Makuta's threats have been defeated."

Pohatu nodded. The six of them had battled a series of enemies sent by Makuta, but all had fallen before the power of the Toa. The island was peaceful, with no threat in sight. Why would a Seventh Toa be needed now?

"Who can fathom the wisdom of Mata

Nui?" Pohatu mused aloud. "I am simply happy to take good news to the north."

"Will you travel with Gali?" Tahu asked, glancing around for the Toa of Water. But Gali was nowhere in sight.

Pohatu smiled. "No," he said. "She has gone to ponder her great thoughts."

Gali sat at the edge of the Amaja Circle, the sacred storytelling area that was part of the island's main temple, the Kini-Nui.

What can it mean? she wondered. *How can it be? A Seventh Toa . . . It's nothing any of us ever imagined. . . .*

At that moment a constellation caught her eye. Six stars gleamed brightly, overpowering the light of the weaker stars all around them.

Suddenly a new point of light, even brighter than the rest, sailed through the constellation. Gali gasped.

"A seventh star!"

UNLEASHED

Deep beneath the island's surface, where no hint of light had ever penetrated, lay the lair of Makuta. Only his glowing red eyes and the shadowy outline of his hulking form were visible as he stalked around his lair.

"The earth shudders, my brother," he rumbled, speaking to the enormous mask on one wall of the chamber, a carved image of the face of the Great Spirit, Mata Nui. "The Seventh Toa has begun its approach." He sighed. "Again the prophecies of the Matoran oppose my will."

Makuta paced restlessly, clutching a stone tablet in one hand. The Toa were about to interfere with his plans. And this time, he intended to defeat them once and for all.

He paused beside three massive carved

stone pillars. The pictographs on them showed
the masks of those who served Makuta's brother,
the Great Spirit, Mata Nui. Makuta touched a
pillar lightly.

"Has it come to this?" he mused. "Must I
release those who should never see the light of
day?"

Makuta plunged his hand into his chest.
When he pulled it out, it clutched three writhing,
snakelike creatures. The kraata.

"I must strike the foundation of the Matoran soul," Makuta hissed. "Their unity can be
poisoned."

He slapped one of the kraata onto the first
pillar. A beam of dark energy burst from the pillar as chunks of stone crumbled and crashed to
the floor. Gradually, a dark, terrifying figure appeared from the rubble. A Rahkshi. The Rahkshi's
body quivered with energy. Dark eyes burned behind the ghastly mask, eyes filled with ruthless
determination.

Makuta smiled grimly. *Welcome, Lerahk, the*

Poison-Rahkshi, he thought. *Your stinger full of deadly poison will sicken anything it contacts.*

He moved on to the next pillar. "Their duty will be broken," he murmured as he slapped on another kraata.

As the kraata burrowed its way into the creature at the heart of the pillar, a long, sinewy blue leg burst out of the stone. With a burst of dark energy, the pillar collapsed, revealing a second Rahkshi. Its eyes glowed. Its limbs twitched with energy.

The Disintegrator-Rahkshi, Guuhrahk, Makuta thought with pride. *Your disintegrator beam has the power to crack any structure.*

Makuta stepped over to the third column. "And their destiny," he whispered, "I must shatter."

He slapped a third kraata onto the column. With a deafening roar, the column shattered. A brown Rahkshi burst through the stone.

Panrahk, the Fragmenter-Rahkshi, Makuta thought. *The arc of your dark energy will cause anything in its path to explode into pieces.*

Makuta stepped back from his creations as a door split open at one end of the chamber.

"Go, my sons," Makuta told them. "Use the shadows." He glanced at the mask of Mata Nui with grim resolve burning in his eyes. "And keep my brother asleep."

A NEW THREAT

Jaller faced Hahli, gathering his courage to say what he wanted before leaving on his quest.

Hahli cleared her throat. "Look, don't get mushy, Jaller," she said. "I have no time for long good-byes."

"I was just going to say . . ." Jaller took a deep breath. "You owe me a rematch on the kolhii field."

Hahli's eyes softened.

"Well then, you'd better hurry back," she said. "'Cause I'll be practicing." She touched him on the arm, then turned and walked away.

Jaller watched her go. How long would it be until he saw her again? *Would* he see her again? Trying not to think about that, he joined Takua on Pewku's back.

"The shadows of the Makuta are powerful," Turaga Vakama warned before they could leave. "Do not take your journey lightly. It will tolerate none of your foolery."

"How will we know where to start?" Takua asked Vakama.

"Trust in the mask," he replied. "Let it be your guide."

Jaller pulled the Mask of Light out of his bag, holding it up. As he turned it in one particular direction, it suddenly began to glow brightly.

"Hard to argue with that," Jaller said.

Takua tapped Pewku's shell and the Ussal galloped off.

Turaga Vakama's voice floated after them. "Remember your duty!" he called. "And walk in the light!"

Gali was still meditating in the Amaja Circle, gazing outward toward the surface of the temple pond.

Suddenly the bright sunlight was cut by a dark shadow. Thick gray clouds were rolling across the sky, turning ordinary day to eerie twilight.

Gali stood and made her way to a plateau overlooking the entire temple. What was happening? As she gazed down at the suva dome, there was a sizzle of energy. An instant later, the suva exploded into a million shards.

A claw reached out of the smoky hole where the suva dome had stood. A moment later three horrifying figures climbed out of the hole and stood surveying the destruction.

Gali gasped. One of the figures swiveled his head in her direction. It banged its staff on the ground, sending sparks of dark energy arcing up. A zigzag lightning bolt shot into the air.

Gali somersaulted backward off the plateau. A split second later, the energy bolt struck the spot where she had stood.

The three Rahkshi climbed higher, seeking their target. But Gali was nowhere to be seen. Hissing with frustration, the trio gave up. The Rahkshi floated upward on the force of their dark energy, hovering over the ground. They flew away, disappearing from the temple area.

A moment later the still surface of the

temple pond rippled, and Gali emerged. She had no idea what sort of creatures they were, but one thing was obvious — they did *not* come in peace.

She glanced down the mountain. Her eyes widened as she spotted the Rahkshi in the distance, hovering purposefully along.

"Ta-Koro!" Gali murmured in alarm.

Diving back beneath the water, she swam in the direction of Tahu's village, determined to warn him in time.

As the river she was following flowed around the base of the Mangai volcano, she took to the land, her wet feet leaving steaming footprints in her wake.

"Why have I been summoned?" Tahu said impatiently as he leaped onto the village wall. He glanced down and spotted Gali.

Before she could answer his question, thunder rumbled in the distance. A huge dark cloud rolled over the village, obscuring the sun.

On the far side of the lake, the three Rahkshi

appeared, seeming to shimmer through the heat rising off the lava. They hovered over the ground, moving smoothly toward the Lake of Fire.

Turaga Vakama had been summoned by the guards as well. He had brought along Turaga Nokama, who had lingered in the village after the kolhii tournament. The two of them squinted into the hazy heat.

"Rahkshi," Nokama pronounced grimly. "The sons of Makuta!"

Vakama nodded. "Shadows that cower in the depths. Exactly as foretold."

Tahu leaped off of the wall. "None have breached Ta-Koro's gates before," he proclaimed. "And none shall this day!"

The Rahkshi didn't even pause at the edge of the lava lake — but merely floated on, moving as easily over the fiery surface as they had over the solid ground.

Tahu blinked in surprise. Then he pulled out his magma swords, holding them at the ready.

As the Rahkshi reached the shore, the Fragmenter raised its staff. A lightning bolt of dark energy arced from its end, zigzagging toward Tahu.

The Fire Toa reacted quickly. A red shield appeared around him an instant before the bolt reached him. The bolt of dark energy hit the shield with awesome power, sending the Toa flying backward through the gates and into the village courtyard.

"Mata Nui protect us!" Vakama cried in horror.

Tahu slid to a stop, dazed. *My shield*, he thought blearily. *What happened? Why didn't it deflect that bolt? What sort of enemy is this?*

His thoughts faded as he slipped into unconsciousness.

DESTRUCTION

The Rahkshi hovered through the wrecked gates and into the village. Suddenly Gali dropped into view from atop the village wall, her aqua axes at the ready.

She looked up at the Rahkshi as the Disintegrator-Rahkshi swung its staff toward her.

She blocked the blow with her axes, then grabbed for the staff, trying to yank it out of its owner's hand. But the Disintegrator was too strong. Gali went flying, tumbling to the ground.

The Disintegrator-Rahkshi touched its staff to the courtyard wall. A shimmer of dark energy poured into the wall, and cracks spread outward like a spiderweb, moving through the structure with awesome speed. The village guards barely had time to leap off before a huge portion of the wall collapsed into a heap of stone debris.

The Disintegrator stepped closer, scanning the wreckage. Meanwhile the Poison-Rahkshi twirled its staff, then poked the stinger end into the ground. Poison flowed out of it, turning the earth a sickly yellow-green.

Tahu was finally regaining his senses. He sat up just in time to see the Fragmenter-Rahkshi walk by, scanning left and right as it went. As Tahu watched, the creature pointed its staff toward a lavastone hut, blasting it into pieces. Approaching the wreckage, the Fragmenter poked at it with the staff, shifting through it.

"Rahkshi!"

The creature turned at Tahu's bold shout. The Toa's swords burned with flames as he spun them and then planted them in the ground at his feet. Twin streaks of fire shot out of them, racing along the ground toward the Rahkshi. Splitting apart when they reached the creature, they formed a wall of flame around it.

Tahu approached warily. He jumped in surprise as the Rahkshi suddenly stepped out through the flames, unharmed.

The Toa and Rahkshi fought furiously. Tahu was matching the creature blow for blow — for now. But he could feel its fearsome power. How long could he stand against it?

The Disintegrator-Rahkshi slammed its staff into the wall near what had once been the village gate. Dark energy spidered through the columns and stones. The Rahkshi turned away, preparing to retreat. But Gali blocked the way.

The Water Toa held her axes crossed in front of her. A geyser of water erupted from the earth, beneath the Rahkshi's feet. The creature raised its staff in defense, but it was too late. The hard ground dissolved into sticky mud, and the Rahkshi's weight made it sink quickly until its feet were trapped.

The Disintegrator hissed angrily, fighting to free itself. Suddenly there was a rumble from behind it. The Rahkshi looked up in alarm — just as the gate wall tumbled onto it, burying it beneath a shower of rubble.

Satisfied that the Rahkshi was trapped — for the moment, at least — Gali turned away. She saw Tahu across the courtyard, locked in battle with the Fragmenter-Rahkshi.

Tahu was fighting hard. He managed to trick the Rahkshi with a false move, then flipped it onto the ground. Then he planted his magma swords in the ground. The earth beneath the Rahkshi split open and lava bubbled up. Tahu leaped away as the Fragmenter sank out of sight.

Hearing someone approach, Tahu glanced over to see Gali hurrying toward him. When he turned his gaze back to the lava pit, he was shocked to see the Fragmenter pulling its way out, dripping with lava but undamaged.

Gali saw the terrible sight, too. "We must get the Matoran to safety — now."

Tahu frowned. "Retreat? *Surrender?*"

"This battle is lost, Tahu!" Gali insisted as

the Fragmenter stepped free of the lava. "We need to regroup!"

Tahu growled. But he realized that Gali was right. "So be it."

Suddenly a familiar voice rang out. "Back, you foul creature!" Vakama cried.

Tahu and Gali exchanged a glance, then raced toward the sound of the Turaga's voice. They arrived to find Vakama weakly waving his firestaff, trying to hold off the Poison-Rahkshi.

"Well done, wise one!" Tahu called to him, leaping forward. "I'll take it from here."

Gali jumped forward to join him. She sent a blast of water toward the Poison-Rahkshi. But the creature dodged at the last moment, and the blast hit Tahu, knocking him off of his feet.

"Brother!" Gali cried out. She watched in horror as the creature loomed over the fallen Tahu, striking at him with its staff. But Tahu somersaulted away, then knocked the Rahkshi's legs out from under it. The creature crashed to the ground and tumbled down to the base of the wall.

Tahu landed on his feet, then dropped to his knees. A faint greenish-brown scratch glowed on the surface of his mask, then faded and disappeared as if it had never been.

Gali rushed up to the Fire Toa. "Tahu, I'm sorr —" she began.

"It's nothing," Tahu cut her off.

He grabbed Vakama as the Poison-Rahkshi planted its staff into the wall beside him. The Toa leaped away just ahead of the poison that was already spreading outward from the wall.

Gali, Tahu, Vakama, and Hahli stood together on the shore, watching as the entire village sank into the lava. The Rahkshi hovered away, disappearing into the steam on the far side.

Tahu took a deep breath. Ta-Koro was no more. But as he glanced around at the crowds of Matoran huddled nearby, he realized that the entire population of the village had escaped.

"They could have destroyed us," he said. "Why didn't they?"

Turaga Vakama shook his head. "They are

seekers," he said. "Whatever they came for they did not find."

"So what were they after?" Gali asked.

"Makuta fears for his spell of shadows," Vakama replied.

Gali and Tahu exchanged a glance. "The Mask of Light!" Gali said, suddenly understanding.

"Then they seek the Seventh Toa," Tahu said. Suddenly realizing what that meant, he gasped. "Jaller and Takua!"

"We'll summon the Toa to find them," Gali said.

Tahu stopped her. "Don't trouble the others, sister," he said. "I will see to their safety myself."

Gali was surprised. "No, Tahu," she said. "We must remain united."

Tahu turned away from her. For an instant, a sickly yellowish-brown glow flashed through his eyes. Then it was gone. He sighed and turned back to Gali.

"If you insist," he said.

DEEP IN THE JUNGLE

Deep in the jungle of Toa Lewa's home region of Le-Wahi, a trio of figures wandered slowly, dwarfed by the ancient trees.

Takua glanced around from his vantage point on Pewku's back. "I hate the jungle," he said. "It's all sticky and" — he paused to slap at something on his neck — "full of bugs."

"How can you say that?" Jaller exclaimed. "It's incredible! Geez, is there any place on Mata Nui where you *do* feel at home?"

"I don't complain about Ta-Koro."

"But you wander off every chance you get, looking for stories," Jaller reminded his friend. "What about *your* story?"

"I don't have a story," Takua insisted with a shrug.

"Only 'cause you won't stand still long enough to make one," Jaller said. "We all have a destiny, you know."

"You know me," Takua said lightly. "Always different."

Suddenly a fierce roar blasted through the jungle. Pewku stopped short, trembling.

Takua gulped. "Yet another reason to hate the jungle," he whispered. "Go that way, Pewku!"

Pewku changed direction. The Mask of Light, which Jaller was still holding, began to fade.

"No," Jaller said. "The mask says this way. Back on track, Pewku." He waited, but the Ussal continued in the new direction. "Pewku!"

Pewku whined nervously. Slowly, she turned back to the original track.

The Ussal stepped forward. She blinked as something — a large shape, blurred with speed — passed in front of them.

Takua didn't notice. "Will you stop with the duty thing and use your head?" he said to Jaller. "Or do you *want* to be jungle snacks?"

"Guess I should listen to the real Herald,"

Jaller retorted sarcastically. He smacked himself in the forehead. "No, wait! You weaseled out. So *I'm* in charge."

Pewku stopped short as a fierce-looking creature stepped out in front of them. It was an ash bear, all teeth and claws.

Takua noticed it. "Fine," he told Jaller, his voice shaking slightly as he pointed to the ash bear. "You're doing great so far."

The ash bear let out a mighty roar. Takua, Jaller, and Pewku shrieked in response. Takua and Jaller ducked as the ash bear's claws swatted at them. Pewku turned and fled, scampering behind a large tree.

The ash bear lunged around the tree in pursuit. Pewku changed direction, heading back the other way around the tree's trunk. But the ash bear was too quick, blocking their way once more. It swiped at them again, missing by the merest fraction. Its claws met the tree trunk instead, leaving deep gashes in the bark.

"Keep him busy!" Jaller said, grabbing the trunk and starting to climb. "I'm . . ."

"Running away and leaving me!" Takua finished for him.

The ash bear made another lunge, backing Takua and Pewku against the tree. Jaller swung up onto a branch directly overhead.

"Just watch!" he called down to his friends. "Toa Tahu does this!"

He jumped out of the tree — right onto the ash bear's broad back. But he'd misjudged his leap and wound up facing the creature's hind-quarters. The ash bear turned away from Takua and Pewku. It grunted and roared angrily as it leaped and twisted, trying to dislodge Jaller.

Takua and Pewku raced out of range. "Toa Tahu does *that?*" Takua muttered, turning to watch as Jaller hung on for dear life.

"Whoa!" Jaller cried, feeling his grasp slip. He had to hold on! If he fell off now . . .

Before he could finish the thought, a sudden gust of vine swirled through the leaves. At the same time, a vine snaked out of the brush, coiling around the ash bear's front foot.

The ash bear growled in surprise as another vine followed the first, wrapping around the creature's back feet and looping them together. The vines tightened, and the ash bear was hoisted off the jungle floor. Jaller finally lost his grip and crashed to the ground, landing face-first.

"Oof!" he grunted.

A tall green figure dropped down out of the foliage above.

"Toa Lewa!" Takua cried.

He bowed to the Toa, while Jaller rolled painfully to a sitting position. Lewa grinned.

"Mata Nui!" he exclaimed to Jaller. "Where'd you learn to bearfight like that, little man?"

Jaller rubbed his sore back. "Right here," he said with a groan.

Lewa playfully grabbed Jaller, setting him gently on his feet. "Well, I'd say you're a natural, brave firespitter," the Toa said.

He released the vines, lowering the ash bear to the ground. The ash bear immediately leaped up and growled.

Takua and Jaller stepped back, leaving Lewa

alone to face the ash bear. The Toa spoke soothingly to the creature. "Go on now, sisterbear."

The ash bear hesitated. Then she turned and lumbered off into the jungle.

Jaller and Takua were amazed. But now that the ash bear was gone, Lewa had other things on his mind. "Word is deepwood that you seek the Seventh Toa," he said.

Takua gestured toward Jaller. "He seeks, I follow. He's the Herald. I'm just his biographer."

Jaller scowled at Takua, but Lewa didn't notice. "If Toa Lewa helped on your search, might he be a spiritlift?"

Takua and Jaller glanced at each other in amazement. The mighty Toa wanted to travel with *them?*

"You?" Takua said. "With us?"

"We'd be honored to have you walk with us!" Jaller added eagerly.

Lewa glanced upward. "Walk?" he said. "Not never! If you ride with me, there'll be no footwalkin' . . ."

There was a *whoosh* from overhead. A

giant, hawklike Gukko bird swooped out of the trees and hovered above them. Lewa grinned at the two Matoran.

"Just airflyin'," he finished. "Ever windfly a Gukko bird?"

Jaller shook his head, his eyes wide. But Takua shrugged. "I've been a second," he said. "But I've never flown one myself."

Lewa grabbed Takua and Jaller and tossed them up onto the Gukko. They landed sitting right behind the bird's head, with Takua in the front.

"Then today's for quicklearnin'," Lewa declared as the Matoran yelped in surprise. "Stay sharp, and follow-well!" He spread his arms, the air katana blades he carried locking into his shoulders. Then he leaped into the air.

As the Gukko wheeled to follow the Toa, Takua glanced down and noticed Pewku watching anxiously from the ground. "Sorry, Pewku," he called to her gently. "No room. Go on home."

Pewku's head drooped sadly. She let out a

soft whine as the Gukko bird flapped through the treetops and disappeared.

Takua and Jaller soon got the hang of following the Gukko's movements as it swooped and glided through the air after Lewa. "Hey, I'm good at this!" Takua cried out as the bird dove through a grove of trees. Takua ducked just in time, but Jaller ended up with a mouthful of leaves.

He spit them out. "As compared to what?" he asked Takua.

The Gukko veered again. Nearby, Lewa did an amazing loop-the-loop in midair, then swooped over to glide along beside the bird and its passengers. "Ha!" the Toa exclaimed. "I was so eager to join your search, I forgot I'm not the wayfinder. Herald, do the honors!"

Jaller raised the mask. It glowed brightly, leading them up through the jungle canopy and over the treetops toward the steep, snow-covered peaks of the Ko-Wahi region, where Kopaka's people made their home.

Soon they reached a snowy plateau. In the background, sheer cliffs rose into ice-covered peaks. The Gukko glided to a landing, stopping abruptly as its feet touched down. Taken by surprise, Takua and Jaller flipped forward over its head, landing face-first in the snow.

Jaller sat up and glared at Takua. Takua shrugged. "What?" he said. "We're here."

Jaller raised the Mask of Light and spun slowly in place. The mask brightened as he faced a ravine between two snowcapped peaks.

"Hey!" Jaller said to Takua in surprise as the Gukko flew off. "You even kept us on the right path. Not bad for a kolhii-head."

He glanced around, looking for Lewa. The Toa was standing at the cliff's edge, looking out over the jungle with an expression of concentration. As Takua and Jaller stepped toward him, they heard the faint sound of tribal drums in the distance.

Lewa turned toward them, looking unusually solemn. "The drums of Le-Koro bring a sorrybad story," he told them. "Your village has . . . fallen. To Rahkshi, the Makuta sons."

Jaller could hardly believe his ears. "My village, in trouble?" he cried, stricken. "I should have been there! I must return!"

"Sorry, firespitter," Lewa said gently. "Pastlate to help now. The mask most needs you."

Jaller turned, shoving the mask into Takua's hands. "Takua will continue in my place."

"Uh-uh, no way!" Takua said quickly. "You accepted this duty."

"I accepted *your* duty!" Jaller shot back.

"Stop!" Lewa ordered sternly. He stepped between them. "What's this dutyquarrel? We *all* have a duty to Mata Nui. No time to infight."

Takua and Jaller exchanged a guilty glance. "I must go be with the Toa," Lewa said. "But then I'll go to your village, Jaller. Heartpromise."

Jaller bowed to the Air Toa. "I . . . can't thank you enough, Toa."

Lewa leaped into the air and glided out of sight. Jaller grabbed the mask back from Takua and headed for the ravine. Takua shrugged and followed.

10

LOST

Dark storm clouds gathered over the mountain peaks as Jaller and Takua struggled through the snowdrifts. On a ridge overlooking the valley, a dark shape watched their progress. Jaller and Takua never noticed it as they clambered through the icy drifts.

Takua paused as the whirling snow cleared just long enough to offer him a glimpse of an odd-looking stone with writing carved on it. "Stop!" he called breathlessly to Jaller. "Does something look familiar here?"

"You mean besides everything?" Jaller panted, gazing around at the whiteout conditions.

"I mean *this*." Takua pointed at the stone. "We've passed this at least a million times. And look . . ." He pointed again, this time to footprints in the snow leading off ahead of them. "Those are either our footprints or the steps to a Le-Matoran dance."

"Well, don't blame me!" Jaller said. "I'm following the mask."

"Fine! Let's all freeze to death because the mask says to," Takua retorted.

Jaller turned and kept walking. Neither he nor Takua noticed as the mask gradually dimmed. "Well, *maybe* our path would be straighter if the *real* Herald had the mask," Jaller snapped.

"The real Herald *has* the mask," Takua returned. "I couldn't find water if I fell out of a canoe."

"Well, what do you think *I* can find?" Jaller said. "I — *oof*!"

His words cut off as he slammed into a tall white figure, almost hidden in the blowing snow.

Takua's eyes widened as the ominous shapes of six white creatures towered over them. "Uh, so far you're good at big scary . . . *Bohrok*!"

Jaller's heart was pounding with fright. The Bohrok were among the most terrifying creatures ever to threaten Mata Nui. But these . . . why did they just stand there, as still as the mountain itself?

"Frozen," he murmured as he realized the truth. "What could do this to them?"

Suddenly one of the Bohrok lurched forward. Jaller and Takua jumped in fright. The Bohrok crashed to the ground . . . revealing a very different figure standing behind it.

"Kopaka!" Jaller exclaimed. "Toa of Ice! H-how did you find us?"

"It was *you* who were following me," Kopaka replied, his icy voice full of suspicion.

Jaller kept a nervous eye on the Toa's ice blade. "We were?" Jaller said.

Kopaka finally put his blade away. He turned and walked off without another word.

Takua and Jaller exchanged a glance. Both were thinking the same thing — the Toa of Ice would make a very useful guide in this frozen wasteland. They hurried after him.

"We didn't mean to," Takua called after

Kopaka, struggling to keep up with him in the deep snow. "We were lost."

"We're on a mission!" Jaller added, holding up the Mask of Light. "We've been sent to find the Seventh Toa," he said, the words tumbling out of him eagerly. "You see, Takua here was in the tunnel where the lava break is, where he's not *supposed* to be, by the way, and I told him —"

Kopaka halted, silencing him with an up-raised hand.

"Ulp," Jaller blurted. "Sorry."

"You are the Chronicler," Kopaka said to Takua.

Takua was a bit unnerved by the Toa's icy gaze. "Uh, yes," he stammered.

Kopaka looked thoughtful. "Your stories have aided the Toa in the past," he said. "I will take you to my village of Ko-Koro. State your purpose to the Turaga."

He strode off, not bothering to look and see if they were following.

*   *   *

At the main temple, Lewa glided to a landing in front of Tahu and Gali. He held up his fist, which Tahu clanked with his own in greeting.

"Ta-Koro is gone, Lewa," Tahu said heavily. "Buried by the very lava that sustained it."

Gali's gaze rested on Tahu. She reached out to touch the scratch on his mask, which appeared to be spreading. "Tahu . . ." she began.

Tahu brushed away her hand. "You worry about scratches?" he said angrily to Gali. "My village is *gone*! Your power was nothing! My power was . . ." He sighed in defeat. "Nothing."

Lewa put a hand on Tahu's shoulder. "We are samehearted, brother. And that heart will quicken us to stop the evilspread."

"But first we must be united," Gali said. "Together we are strong."

Without answering either of them, Tahu turned and stalked away.

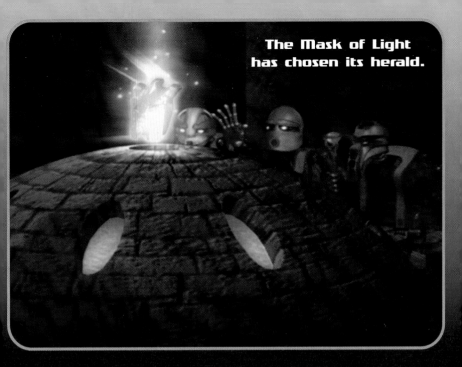

The Mask of Light
has chosen its herald.

Turaga Vakama will not allow
Jaller to escape his duty.

Takua and Jaller set off on their dangerous quest to find the Seventh Toa.

Vakama reminds the young Matoran to trust in the mask — it will lead them to their destiny.

Gali meditates on the strange significance of the Mask of Light. Could there really be a Seventh Toa?

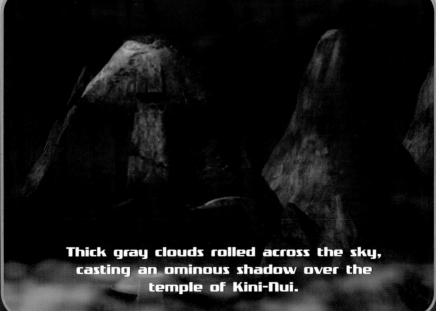

Thick gray clouds rolled across the sky, casting an ominous shadow over the temple of Kini-Nui.

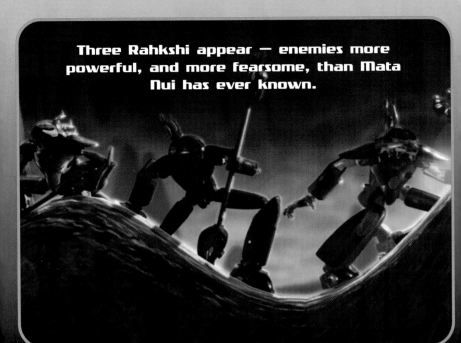

Three Rahkshi appear — enemies more powerful, and more fearsome, than Mata Nui has ever known.

Will the Rahkshi prove too powerful for even the Toa'Nuva?

Kopaka and Lewa do everything they can
to rescue Tahu from the Rahkshi's poison.

The time for running is over. The Toa
Nuva are ready to stand their ground.

Takua mourns Jaller, who has finally
discovered his tragic destiny.

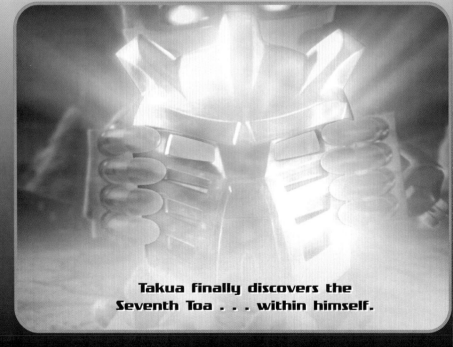

Takua finally discovers the
Seventh Toa . . . within himself.

Having failed their mission,
the Rahkshi fall to their knees.

Takanuva will stop at
nothing to defeat Makuta.

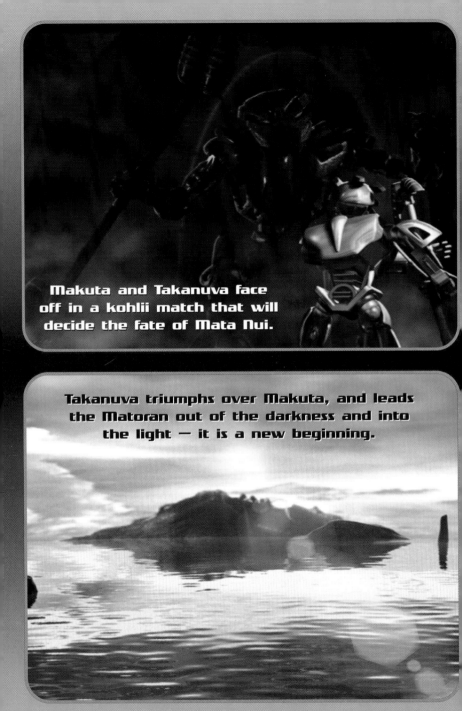

Makuta and Takanuva face off in a kohlii match that will decide the fate of Mata Nui.

Takanuva triumphs over Makuta, and leads the Matoran out of the darkness and into the light — it is a new beginning.

DEEP FREEZE

Takua, Jaller, and Kopaka rounded a hill of ice. Before them spread a snowy valley. Steep cliffs rose on the far side. Set into one of the cliffs was a village, accessible only by a bridge of ice.

But something was wrong. The village wall had fallen. Huts were in a shambles, and smoke rose from the ruins. There was no one in sight.

Jaller and Takua raced toward the ice bridge, wanting to help.

Kopaka glanced up as a dark shadow fell over the valley. "Stop!" he shouted.

Takua and Jaller skidded to a halt. The bridge was just ahead, stretching over a deep chasm. From below the lip of the gorge, three terrifying figures hovered into view.

The trio of Rahkshi landed in front of the awestruck Matoran, unfolding their legs to stand at full height. Takua and Jaller goggled up at the hideous creatures, frozen with fear.

The Fragmenter-Rahkshi planted its staff in the snow. A zigzagging bolt arced into the air, then down toward the helpless pair.

Kopaka slid toward them, his shield up. The ice shield deflected the bolt, its energy knocking the Toa backward. The bolt blasted back toward the Rahkshi, shooting a plume of snow into the air as the creatures dove for safety.

The Fragmenter let out an angry roar. Kopaka climbed to his feet and raced away with Takua and Jaller close behind him. The Rahkshi chased them, launching bolt after bolt of energy, which rained down all around the fleeing trio.

Suddenly Kopaka stopped short, flinging out his blade to block the Matoran's path. Takua and Jaller slid to a stop, realizing that they were about to race right off of a steep cliff that dropped away into a treacherous ravine.

"Prepare," Kopaka ordered, turning to face their pursuers.

Jaller and Takua blinked, confused, as the Toa tossed his shield facedown onto the snow beside them. Suddenly realizing what Kopaka meant for them to do, Jaller shook his head. "The Captain of the Guard never runs awaaaaaaay!"

His last word was lost in a cry of terror as Takua pushed him onto the shield and jumped aboard himself. The momentum carried the shield skidding toward the cliff. It toppled on the edge, then tipped down, sliding faster and faster along the impossibly steep incline.

Kopaka hardly heard their fading screams. He faced the Rahkshi as they closed in on him.

The Fragmenter-Rahkshi sent yet another bolt of energy arcing toward him. Kopaka somersaulted away, dodging the bolt. As he came down, he tossed his twin blades onto the snow. He landed on them, turning them into power ice skates, on which he glided down the cliff face.

The Rahkshi watched him go, their burning eyes sparking with anger.

*   *   *

Jaller clutched the edge of the shield-sled, now too terrified to scream. The shield sped down the cliff at an awesome speed.

He was relieved to see Kopaka appear beside them. As they neared the bottom of the slope, Takua pointed ahead. "Dead end!" he cried.

The base of the cliff sloped into a sheer rock face. Only a narrow ravine leading to a small lake offered a path through.

Kopaka zoomed ahead of the shield. Bending his knees, he reached back and grabbed the front edge, pulling it behind him as he veered into the ravine.

"Whoaaaaa!" Takua and Jaller yelled as they felt themselves skid up the ravine wall.

But Kopaka yanked the shield back onto the icy path. They sped down the ravine.

BOOM! An arc of dark energy smashed into the snow right in Kopaka's path. The shock waves knocked him off his feet, sending him rolling into the snow.

The shield flipped over, dumping Takua and

Jaller as well. They tumbled head over heels, landing on the very edge of the lake.

The Fragmenter-Rahkshi hissed triumphantly as it hovered down toward him. The other two Rahkshi were right behind the first.

Takua sat up. "Jaller?" he said.

Jaller looked at him, his eyes widening as he spotted the Rahkshi. The creatures hovered right past Kopaka, who appeared to be unconscious, heading straight for the two Matoran.

"Why us?" Jaller said. "What did *we* do?"

Takua spotted the Mask of Light in his friend's hand. "The mask!" he cried. He grabbed the mask, which started glowing brighter than ever. Pushing Kopaka's shield onto the cold water of the lake, he jumped on, using the mask as a paddle.

Left behind, Jaller watched nervously as the Rahkshi approached. He dove out of the way as they hovered toward him. But they didn't even glance his way. Their glowing eyes were focused on Takua. They hovered out over the water, following him.

Takua paddled as hard as he could. But with

every glance back, he saw the Rahkshi gaining on him. Finally they were close enough to reach out for him with their clawed arms.

Takua held the mask close to his chest as the creatures hissed threateningly, grabbing at him. *I guess this is it*, he thought hopelessly as a clawed hand snapped only a whisper away from his face.

Just then his gaze caught motion back on the lakeshore. Kopaka was awake — he was swinging his ice blade overhead. A second later a blast of elemental ice spun through the air, heading straight for the Rahkshi!

The icy blast hit the Fragmenter-Rahkshi and knocked it off balance. It crashed into the other two creatures, and all three of them toppled and landed in the lake with a splash.

"Ha!" Takua cried excitedly, leaning over the edge of the shield to look at the spot where the Rahkshi had disappeared.

A clawed hand shot up, only inches from his face.

"Yaaaa!" Takua yelped, pulling his head back.

Kopaka twirled his blade, then stabbed the point into the edge of the lake. The water crystallized instantly into ice, the deep freeze spreading rapidly until the entire lake was frozen solid. The Rahkshi, who were just reaching the surface, were trapped in place.

Kopaka and Jaller walked out onto the ice. "Good moves," Kopaka said when they reached Takua.

Takua shrugged. "Even I get lucky sometimes," he said, a little awed by the words of praise from the Toa.

"Not luck," Kopaka corrected. "It is what you *do* that makes a hero."

There was a sound from behind them. All three whirled around to look.

"Pewku!" Takua cried in amazement as he saw the familiar form of the Ussal crab trotting across the ice.

Pewku ran toward him. Her feet skidded on the slippery ice, and she wound up crashing into Takua, knocking him over.

Takua laughed and hugged her. "Wow!" he

said. "She must have come all the way through the jungle."

"Not bad," Jaller said with a smile. "Maybe Pewku should be the Herald, eh, Toa Kopaka?"

He turned to glance at the Toa. But the spot where Kopaka had been standing just a moment before was empty. The Toa was back on the shore, leaping up the sheer face of the icy cliff.

Jaller blinked. "He just left us here!"

Takua nodded, remembering the distressing view of Ko-Koro. "He needs to see his village." He held the Mask of Light toward his friend. "Here."

Jaller started to reach for it, then hesitated. "You were looking pretty Herald-like back there. Sure you don't want to hang on to it?"

Takua slapped the mask against Jaller's chest. "Tempting," he said as the mask's glow slowly faded. "But no."

THE DECISION

A few hours later, Takua, Jaller, and Pewku stopped beside a small tunnel entrance dug out of an icy mountainside. Takua leaned closer to read the writing on a battered old totem that marked the entrance.

"Onu-Koro," he read. He glanced at Jaller. "It doesn't look like it's been used in a while. And we don't have a lightstone."

Jaller held up the faintly glowing mask. "Who needs lightstones?"

He led the way into the tunnel. Pewku followed. Takua hesitated, then climbed down into the darkness after them.

The tunnels were too low to allow the Matoran to ride Pewku, so all three of them walked along on foot. Takua was lagging behind.

He didn't want to admit it, but being underground made him nervous. It was too still. Too close. And much, much too dark.

Takua . . .

Takua stopped short. Was he hearing things? He peered into the darkness behind him. But there was no sign of life or movement.

By the time he turned around, Jaller and Pewku had disappeared.

"Uh, guys?" Takua called. "Where'd you go?"

Takua . . .

Takua gulped. That time he'd definitely heard it. But who? Where? Why?

He wasn't sure he wanted to know the answer. "J-Jaller?" he called, racing forward. "JALLER! *Oof*—"

In the blinding dark, he crashed into a wall and fell.

Suddenly an eerie red glow lit up the tunnel. A pair of red eyes appeared in the dimness.

"Shadows are everything," a voice hissed. "And where they are, so am I."

Takua backed away from the eyes. His heart was pounding. The Makuta. It had to be. "I know who you are," he said, trying to keep his voice from quavering. "I — I'm not afraid."

"Even my shadows cannot hide your fear," Makuta said. "Or the truth."

"What truth?" Takua asked.

"That you will not find the Seventh Toa. And deep down, you know it."

"So I won't," Takua said uncertainly. "Maybe Jaller will."

"And if he doesn't?" Makuta's voice was more ominous than ever. "He will die, because of you. Bring *me* the mask, Takua. Bring it to me and you won't lose your friend."

Takua was horrified. Was this his choice? Betray all of Mata Nui — or allow Jaller to die?

Makuta is said to be the master of lies, he thought. *Maybe this choice is a lie, too. . . .*

"N-no!" he cried, trying to sound bold and sure. "I won't let everyone down."

"You fail them more if you refuse," Makuta

said. "For the mask, your villages *and* Jaller will be spared. Don't be a fool."

"N-no," Takua stammered, confused. "I can't . . ."

Suddenly a flash of light flooded the tunnel. "Hey!" Jaller's voice called from somewhere ahead. A second later he and Pewku appeared. "Keep up, kolhii-head," Jaller chided. "I found some better tunnels!"

Takua stared around wildly. But there was no sign of Makuta. Unable to speak, he merely nodded and followed as Jaller and Pewku turned and headed down the tunnel again.

"So where'd you wander off to?" Jaller asked over his shoulder as they walked.

"Jaller," Takua said. "Um, about the mask . . ."

"What about it?" Jaller asked. "You ready to take it? *Finally?*"

Takua paused, struggling to make up his mind. "I can't . . ." He took a deep breath. ". . . go with you."

"What?" Jaller exclaimed, clutching the mask, which faded slightly. "Why?"

Takua could only shake his head hopelessly. "I . . . can't explain," he croaked.

Jaller frowned. "Oh, that's just great," he said angrily. "First you stick me with *your* duty and then you ditch me?"

Takua couldn't meet his friend's eyes. "My duty is to myself," he muttered, turning away. "I quit. Just take the mask and go."

At that moment, the last of the mask's light faded. "Fine," Jaller said. At his words, the mask's glow returned — at least a little. "But *I* won't give up. I will find the Seventh Toa, whether you're the true Herald or not."

Pewku stood still, staring first after Takua and then Jaller. She turned and followed Takua.

Makuta watched Takua's retreat from his lair deep beneath the tunnels, his red eyes glowing with anger. "My fairness spurned . . ." he hissed, turning toward the giant mask of Mata Nui on the wall. "My gentle sons bound in ice." He glared at the mask. "So, my hand is cast."

He turned to face three stone pillars,

nearly identical to the ones from which the Rahkshi had emerged. As Makuta walked by them, three shadowy forms burst out of them.

"Now I must pierce that which the Toa hold dear," Makuta said. He stopped in front of one of the new figures — another Rahkshi, this one white in color. Its name was Kurahk — the Anger-Rahkshi. "Anger among them will threaten their precious unity."

Makuta walked on. This time he paused before a Rahkshi that was as black as night. Vorahk — the Hunger-Rahkshi.

"Hunger will consume their duty," Makuta said as the creature's staff quivered with energy.

The third Rahkshi was colored in fearful shades of red. This was Turahk, the Fear-Rahkshi.

"And fear will keep them from their destiny." Makuta turned away from the three new Rahkshi, once again facing the still mask of Mata Nui. "They will not disturb your sleep."

BATTLE

Onua and Pohatu were conferring in the center courtyard of Onu-Koro when they heard steps approaching from one of the tunnels.

Pohatu saw an exhausted-looking Ussal crab trotting toward him. His eyes widened in surprise as he recognized the figure riding atop the Ussal's back.

"Chronicler!" Pohatu exclaimed as Takua and Pewku made their way toward the Toa. "Where is the Herald?"

Takua looked tired and uncertain. "Uh, we got . . . separated," he said. "After we met the Rahkshi."

Onua and Pohatu exchanged a glance. "What is Rahkshi?" Pohatu asked Takua.

Before Takua could answer, the ground shuddered. The villagers around them cried out in alarm. Suddenly the cavern wall burst open — and three tall, horrifying figures leaped into view, hissing angrily.

"Those!" Takua cried, pointing to the Rahkshi. He blinked, realizing that the colors were different. "Except . . . different ones."

"Clear the cave!" Onua shouted. "And close the tunnel behind you!"

The Onu-Matoran scattered, racing for the tunnels leading away from the cavern. Meanwhile Onua and Pohatu faced the three Rahkshi.

"Let me show you a real Onu-Koro welcome," Onua rumbled. He slammed his fists onto the ground, creating an elemental tidal wave of earth and stone. The wave rippled toward the Rahkshi and swallowed them.

But when the wave had passed, the Rahkshi rose up again, unharmed.

Onua grunted in surprise. The Hunger-Rahkshi leaped toward him, wielding its staff. Onua grabbed at the staff, trying to pull it away.

Meanwhile Pohatu raced toward the Fear-Rahkshi. The creature raised its staff, sending dark energy waves rippling out from it. As soon as Pohatu hit the circle of energy, he stopped in midstride, his eyes filled with dark fear.

"No . . ." he whimpered, mesmerized by the overwhelming, inescapable fear. All of his worst fears seemed to be exploding within him. "Water, sinking, drowning . . . !"

The Hunger-Rahkshi hissed at Onua as they struggled over the staff. The creature activated the staff. Dark hunger energy flooded into Onua, instantly draining him of power, channeling it instead back into the Rahkshi's staff.

"My strength," Onua whispered weakly. "My power . . ."

His eyes dimmed and he fell over backward, landing with a mighty crash. He couldn't move — his energy was completely gone, replaced by a gnawing, devastating hunger.

"Onua!" Pohatu cried.

Still imprisoned by a wall of fear, Pohatu was unable to help. And the more he struggled against it, the more the terror overwhelmed him — until, with a final moan of helplessness, he collapsed to the ground.

Takua tried to avoid the fleeing villagers as he and Pewku searched for escape as well. The three Rahkshi turned and spotted him in the crowds. Knocking other Matoran out of the way, they stalked after him with a hiss.

Pewku found her way to a tunnel while the Rahkshi were still halfway back across the large cavern. Takua breathed out in relief. They were going to make it!

Then he turned and saw the scene behind him. The Rahkshi were stomping on huts and shoving aside terrified Onu-Matoran. Onua and Pohatu were still sprawled motionless on the cavern floor.

This is my fault, Takua realized. *They're destroying everything in their path — to get to me.*

His eyes hardened with resolve. Grabbing a kolhii stick that was leaning against a hut nearby, he turned Pewku to face the approaching Rahkshi.

"Yah, Pewku!" he shouted, urging the Ussal onward. "Yah!"

Pewku tried to do as he said. But so many villagers were fleeing, flowing around them in their race for the tunnel, that they could hardly move forward. Finally Takua gave up. Slumping to the ground, he closed his eyes and waited for the Rahkshi to reach him.

Pewku whined frantically, trying to get him to move. But he pushed her claw aside.

"Go find a real hero," he mumbled miserably. "What can I do?"

Tahu, Lewa, and Gali raced through a tunnel, heading toward the main cavern of Onu-Koro. They skidded to a stop as they reached the end of the tunnel and saw the mayhem in the cavern.

Tahu's eyes flashed with anger as he took it in. The poison taint, which had spread to cover half of his face, glowed angrily as well.

He leaped into the cavern without a word. "Tahu!" Lewa cried, grabbing at him. But it was too late.

"RAHKSHI!" Tahu bellowed furiously, racing toward the creatures. He charged at the Anger-Rahkshi first.

The Anger-Rahkshi banged its staff on the ground. A ring of dark energy rippled across the cavern floor, hitting Tahu and knocking him off of his feet.

The Fire Toa landed with a grunt on the hard ground. Gali and Lewa leaped out of the tunnel and raced toward the action. Lewa spotted a small figure huddled on the ground near the Rahkshi.

The Chronicler, he thought in surprise. *And his crab friend, Pewku. Looks like they're in badneed of a rescue.*

He glided toward them, grabbing Takua in one arm and Pewku in the other.

The Rahkshi hissed in frustration as they saw their quarry fly away across the cavern. They turned and stalked after him.

Tahu's eyes glowed dark, anger-energy flashing across them. The poison taint had spread once again and now covered his entire mask.

He leaped to his feet. Gali gasped as she

saw that it wasn't just Tahu's mask that was poisoned now. The taint had spread across his entire body!

The Rahkshi's anger-energy must have caused it to spread more rapidly, she thought in alarm.

She took a step toward him. "Brother!" she said with concern.

"FIRE HAS NO BROTHERS!" Tahu howled. "FIRE CONSUMES ALL!"

He slammed his swords into the ground. Jagged fissures of lava burst into life and tore across the ground in all directions. Gali balanced on a pillar of earth as fire consumed the ground on either side.

Tahu looked at her, but there was no recognition in his eyes — only anger. He slammed his swords down again, sending another fissure of lava right at Gali. She somersaulted away just in time as the ground exploded into flame.

Across the cavern, Lewa glided down and deposited Takua and Pewku beside Onua and Pohatu. "No thought-thinking," the Toa ordered Takua breathlessly. "Quickspeed to Jaller. Warn him!"

"I . . . er . . . will," Takua called as the Air Toa glided away, heading toward Tahu and Gali.

Takua led the way as he and Pewku raced toward an escape tunnel. But a few strides away, the Ussal veered suddenly, heading through a narrow foundry doorway instead.

"Pewku!" Takua cried. "Where are you going?"

He followed her. A moment later, the Rahkshi disappeared through the foundry door as well.

At that moment back in the cavern, Pohatu finally came to and sat up. He glanced at Onua, who was pushing himself upright nearby. "Rise and shine, brother," Pohatu joked weakly.

Onua merely groaned in response.

The heat rolled over Takua in waves as he followed Pewku into the depths of the foundry. Several fires blazed beneath narrow exhaust chimneys cut into the rock ceiling. Mine-cars loaded with lightstones sat on their tracks, waiting to move out.

Dead end, Takua realized as he stared around the chamber. *There's no way out except the way we came . . . and we can't go that way.*

The trio of Rahkshi emerged from the entry tunnel into the foundry chamber with a loud hiss. Pewku raced toward one of the chimneys. She grunted urgently at Takua and leaped up, scrambling for a hold on the rough rock sides.

Takua took a deep breath. What choice did he have? He leaped up, following the Ussal into the soot-blackened chimney.

As he struggled to climb up the chimney, he heard the Rahkshi hissing directly beneath him. He tried to climb faster, but it was no use — the Fear-Rahkshi was right behind him. It lunged up, grabbing for his foot.

BURIED ALIVE

Suddenly a claw spun into view, pinning the Fear-Rahkshi's arm to the wall just before its clawed hand closed around Takua's leg. It was one of Toa Pohatu's mighty climbing claws!

The other two Rahkshi charged toward the Toa. Onua slammed his fists outward into the cavern walls. The section of ceiling directly over the Rahkshi collapsed, piling rocks and stone dust over them.

Breathing a sigh of relief, Takua pulled himself up to safety.

In the courtyard cavern, Tahu swiped his swords at Lewa, who dodged them easily. Tahu lunged at Lewa again.

Rocks rained down on him from the ceiling, mixed with snow. Suddenly a stream of water struck Tahu from behind.

Howling with anger, he turned to find Gali behind him.

"Tahu," she called. "Remember who you are! Remember your destiny." She unleashed another stream of water. Tahu's armor steamed as the cool water hit it.

"I HAVE NO DESTINY!" he roared furiously. "I — agh?"

He jumped in surprise as a shape plummeted to the ground behind him. Kopaka! The Ice Toa touched his blade to the ground. A layer of frost washed over the ground, trapping Tahu in a thick coating of ice.

Lewa stepped forward. He and Kopaka each took one of the frozen Tahu's arms, carrying him toward an exit tunnel.

Gali looked around for the others as she raced after them. She saw Onua's quake-breakers smash through the stone of a collapsed foundry entrance and breathed out with relief as he and Onua emerged into the courtyard chamber.

Lewa and Kopaka carried the unconscious Tahu into a tunnel. Gali followed. Once inside the tunnel, she turned back to check on the others' progress. Pohatu and Onua raced across the chamber toward her. They were steps from safety when there was an ominous rumble. A split second later, the entire cavern collapsed on top of them.

Gali gasped in horror. "Our brothers!" she cried as rocks and earth rained down, burying everything in a deep layer of debris.

She tried to leap out, to go help. But Kopaka stopped her.

He gave her a somber look. Gali returned the look for a long moment, then glanced out at the caved-in courtyard area. There was no sound, no movement except the settling dust.

She bowed her head sadly and turned to follow the others.

With a grunt and a clatter, Pewku pulled herself up and out of the top of the chimney. She fell to the snowy ground outside with a sigh of relief.

A moment later, Takua clambered out after

her. He flopped to the ground, exhausted. He wished he could just lie there, sleeping in the soft snow. But he knew that he couldn't do that.

Pewku grunted questioningly as Takua climbed to his feet. "No time to rest," he told her. "We've got to find Jaller. Come on!"

A short distance away, on the shores of a frozen glacial lake, the setting sun's rays touched the end of a staff protruding out of the ice. As the last light faded and dusk fell, the staff and everything else fell into dark shadow.

For a long moment, nothing moved. Then a flicker of dark energy burst out of the end of the staff. The ice around it splintered and began to crack and melt.

TOGETHER AGAIN

As the sun rose above the horizon, Jaller tried to keep his gaze on his goal — the craggy top section of the Mangai volcano. He struggled up a rocky slope, clutching the Mask of Light.

As he crested the slope, he groaned in dismay. Another steep cliff side still lay between him and the top of the volcano!

His legs ached, and his eyes strained in the bright morning sunlight. Would he be able to make it? And even if he reached the top of the volcano, what then? Would he find the Seventh Toa there — or would the mask lead him off in yet another direction?

"Mata Nui," he cried. "Show me where my destiny lies!"

Suddenly the ground quaked beneath him.

Jaller was thrown off his feet — and off of the ledge. He barely managed to grab onto it and avoid falling.

He sighed and glanced upward, rolling his eyes. "Well," he said to the sky, "I guess I asked!"

The ground shook again. But this time, Jaller realized it was the rumble of galloping footsteps coming toward him.

"What now?" he wondered aloud.

Jaller's eyes widened as Pewku galloped onto the ledge. Takua was riding on her broad back, holding a kolhii stick in one hand.

Takua leaned over Pewku's side, stretching the kolhii stick down toward Jaller. Jaller grabbed it, holding on tightly as his friend pulled him to safety.

Soon Jaller was seated behind Takua on Pewku's back. "What happened to 'I quit'?" he asked breathlessly.

Takua grinned. "I tried that," he said. "But no one will let me." His face grew serious. "Bad news. More Rahkshi. They've taken Onu-Koro."

"The Mask of Light was never at Onu-Koro," Jaller said, confused.

Takua shrugged. "They don't want the mask," he said. "They're looking for the Herald."

Jaller still looked puzzled. "You're sure they were after the Herald?"

Takua glanced at him over his shoulder. "Oh, yes," he said. "*Very* sure."

Tahu roared, struggling to free himself from the vines that trapped him. He crashed from side to side, the large, flat stone beneath him glowing hot with the force of his fury.

"The poison is destroying him," Gali said quietly, watching from nearby.

Lewa and Kopaka stood beside her near a tunnel entrance in the jungle.

"We must act," Gali continued. "Let us summon all the healing powers we possess."

The three of them gathered around Tahu. The Fire Toa hardly seemed aware of their presence as he growled and fought against his restraints.

Lewa raised Tahu's magma swords. They burned weakly, with nothing more than a sputtering flicker.

"His flame is but an emberglow!" Lewa noted in alarm.

"Kopaka," Gali said.

Kopaka produced his own blade. He crossed it with the magma swords in front of Tahu's face. The energy of two Toa's blades exploded in a blinding flash of light, then flowed down into Tahu's body.

Tahu roared defiantly as the energy flooded him. He was soon enveloped in glowing white steam.

"Enough!" Gali cried.

Kopaka and Lewa pulled back the swords. The steam dissipated, revealing Tahu—and the poison taint still covering his body. The Fire Toa lay still, his eyes dark.

"Brother!" Lewa cried, fearing the worst.

Gali brought her hands together. Water droplets rushed together at her call, forming a liquid sphere that spun in front of her. *Liquid of life, do your magic,* she thought, focusing all of her energy on the water's cleansing power.

She unleashed the water at Tahu in a gentle mist. A rainbow formed as the droplets danced over his still form.

The water bathed him, washing away the poison along with the scratch on his mask. Within seconds, healthy red armor shone out.

Gali slumped, exhausted. Kopaka caught her, carefully helping her move away to rest.

Lewa gazed down at Tahu. The Fire Toa still lay motionless, but Lewa could see that Gali's efforts had worked. There was no sign of the poison taint.

Lewa very gently clanked his fist against Tahu's hand. "I'm right here, Toa brother," he murmured.

Gali was kneeling beside a jungle pond. She held her hands beneath the water, taking energy from it. Kopaka stood behind her, watching.

"Kopaka," Gali said with a sigh as she felt herself recharged. "Do you think the Turaga were right about us? Have we lost our unity?" She paused, gazing down at the still water. When the Ice Toa didn't answer, she turned her head. "Kopaka?"

But he was gone. Gali sighed.

Just then Lewa called out for her. "Sister, he is openeyed!"

Gali hurried back to the clearing. Tahu was sitting up, unwrapping the vines from his wrists.

"Brother," Gali greeted him. "Are you well?"

Tahu glared at her. "No, I am not well." Then his eyes softened. "But I am alive and in your debt . . . my sister."

He tentatively lifted his fist toward her. Gali smiled and gently clanked it with her own.

KINI-NUI

Jaller breathed out, awed by the sight that lay before his eyes. "Kini-Nui!" he whispered. "The Great Temple!"

The temple and the surrounding mountains were bathed in the colorful rays of the setting sun. The Mask of Light glowed as they crossed the Amaja Circle. As they approached a giant head carved into the stone at the edge of the plateau, the mask's light faded.

"No way," Takua said. "We've been all over the island, just to wind up here?"

"Why not? It's a sacred place," Jaller pointed out.

Takua grabbed the mask, which immediately glowed brightly again. "You sure you're working this right?"

At that moment a beam of brilliant light shot out of the mask. It landed on the giant stone head. The ground quaked, shaking loose countless years' worth of dirt and grime from the carving. As the outlines of a mask began to be visible underneath, the sun dipped beneath the horizon, plunging the temple into dusky dimness.

"Wow, this is it," Jaller said. "The Seventh Toa must be here."

An ominous hiss rose nearby. Takua and Jaller turned toward the sound in fear. Three Rahkshi stepped out from behind a rock — Fragmenter, Disintegrator, and Poison.

Jaller gasped. "Give me the mask, Takua," he said grimly, grabbing it from his friend's hands.

"Jaller, no!" Takua cried. "We both know the mask chose me. I am the true Herald."

"Are you still sure, even now?"

Takua held out his hand. "Yes!" he said firmly. "I'm the Herald."

Jaller hesitated briefly, then handed over the mask. Takua nodded. "And I say . . . *run!*" he cried.

Takua, Jaller, and Pewku raced down toward the lower plateau. The ground quaked again at the base of the steps. A fissure erupted in a shower of rocks and earth, and three more Rahkshi burst out of the ground!

Takua and Jaller turned to race back up the steps. But the first trio of Rahkshi were already descending from the top. They were trapped!

Suddenly a flare of brilliant fire rocketed overhead, illuminating the entire temple.

The Rahkshi shielded their faces against the glare. An urn atop the enormous stone head ignited, illuminating Lewa and Gali, who stood on either side. Tahu stepped in from the shadows, the fire reflecting off of his bright red armor.

Takua let out a breath of relief. "Great!" he called to the three Toa as they leaped into the air. "You can get us out of here!"

Tahu pulled out his swords. "We are done running."

The Fragmenter-Rahkshi hissed, unleashing an arc of dark energy from its staff. Tahu lifted his shield, enveloping all of the Toa and Matoran in a protective force field. He staggered backward as the Rahkshi's bolt hit, but recovered quickly.

"We will not be broken!" the Fire Toa shouted defiantly.

He and Lewa stood side by side as the Fragmenter-, Poison-, and Disintegrator-Rahkshi approached. Behind them, Gali led Takua and Jaller down the steps toward the lower temple.

"This way!" she cried.

Lewa summoned a whirlwind, sending it spinning down to grab the sand from the Amaja Circle. The sand cycloned feverishly, enveloping the advancing Rahkshi. Tahu crossed his swords, sending a blast of fire into the swirling sandstorm. The sand particles glowed red, then white-hot. When Tahu and Lewa both lowered their arms, their creation remained — the Rahkshi were trapped from the neck down in a prison of glass!

In the lower temple, the other three Rahkshi moved toward Gali and her charges, cutting off their escape. The ground between them suddenly rumbled and exploded. Three figures erupted out of the quake, landing beside Gali and the others.

Gali cried out in amazement as she recognized the Ice, Earth, and Stone Toa. "Brothers!" she shouted to Pohatu and Onua. "We thought we lost you."

"You might have, but for our frosty friend," Onua replied, gesturing toward Kopaka.

Kopaka shrugged. "It was . . . on the way."

Gali raised an eyebrow. "Kopaka had to dig out the chief miner?"

Onua looked sheepish. "Well, he needs to get his hands dirty from time to time."

The Hunger-, Anger-, and Fear-Rahkshi had recovered from the surprise of the Toa's arrival. They advanced again, hissing menacingly.

The Anger-Rahkshi banged its staff on the ground, sending a ring of dark anger energy toward the Toa. But the energy passed right through them, leaving them untouched. The Rahkshi hissed in surprise.

"Our anger is no more, Rahkshi," Tahu said. "We are united!"

Lewa and Pohatu leaped into action, somersaulting around the three Rahkshi faster than the eye could follow. The creatures swung their staffs wildly at their tumbling foes — but wound up striking one another instead!

The Fear-Rahkshi squealed in dismay as the Hunger-Rahkshi's staff hit it. Its fear energy drained from its body, sending it tumbling helplessly to the ground.

The Hunger-Rahkshi hissed. Turning away from the circling Toa, it leaped toward Takua and Jaller. In the blink of an eye, Tahu and Gali joined together and summoned their elemental powers. A blast of steam burst from their tools, catching the Hunger-Rahkshi in its mighty stream and lifting it into the air.

The Toa moved in on the Anger-Rahkshi. The creature backed away, hissing in frustration.

Behind the Toa, the Fear-Rahkshi stirred. Its eyes began to glow as energy flowed back into its body. The creature climbed to its feet and started up the steps toward Takua and Jaller.

The Toa didn't notice. All of their attention

was focused on the Anger-Rahkshi in front of them. "Now," Tahu shouted. "As one!"

The others knew what to do.

Onua slammed the ground, sending a wave of earth toward the Anger-Rahkshi.

Pohatu transformed the rolling wave of earth into a wave of boulders.

Tahu transformed the boulders into a wave of lava, which broke over the Rahkshi, enveloping it.

The Anger-Rahkshi tried to escape the lava. But suddenly the jet of steam dissipated, sending the Hunger-Rahkshi plunging back to earth — right on top of the Anger-Rahkshi!

Kopaka jumped forward, striking the lava with his sword and instantly freezing it solid. Both the Hunger- and Anger-Rahkshi were frozen along with it.

Tahu stepped toward them, examining the Toa's handiwork. "They've been trapped before and were still able to escape," he reminded the others.

Kopaka leaned in, yanking the kraata out of the Rahkshi's armored bodies. "Not this time."

A frightened squeal erupted from somewhere above. Glancing up, the Toa were just in time to see Pewku tumble down the steps, tossed aside by the Fear-Rahkshi. The creature turned with a hiss, backing Takua and Jaller up the steps.

ONE DESTINY

"Hang on!" Gali shouted.

Takua looked down, trying to see the Toa. Instead, his gaze caught the beam of dark fear energy emanating from the Rahkshi's staff. He fell to his knees, instantly transfixed.

The Fear-Rahkshi rose up on its long legs, towering over Takua. It swung its staff toward the helpless Matoran.

But Jaller had seen what was happening. He leaped forward, swinging the kolhii stick he was holding.

Takua snapped out of his fear trance as Jaller intercepted the Rahkshi's blow. "*Jaller!*" he screamed as dark energy sizzled through his friend's body.

The Fear-Rahkshi turned toward him, its

eyes glittering wickedly. But before it could strike again, Gali and Pohatu leaped in and grabbed it by the arms.

Takua dropped the mask, racing over and cradling his fallen friend. "What have you done?" he cried as Jaller's eyes dimmed. "I'm supposed to make the sacrifice! I'm the Herald!"

"No," Jaller said weakly. "The duty was mine. You know . . ." He paused, gathering the last scraps of his fading strength. He took in a ragged breath.

". . . who you are," he whispered faintly. Stretching out his hand, he picked up the Mask of Light and put it in Takua's hands. "You were always different."

Jaller's hand dropped limply onto the stone. Gently lowering his friend's head to the ground, Takua stood, lifting the mask. It glowed more brightly than ever.

Takua stood still for a moment, his eyes distant.

Nearby, the Fear-Rahkshi struggled free of Gali's and Pohatu's grip. The two Toa lost their footing and tumbled down the steps, crashing into the other Toa, who were on their way to help.

Takua turned the mask over in his hands again. His eyes narrowed purposefully. As he lifted it to his face, the mask's glow brightened again. As it made contact with his own mask, it burst forth with brilliant beams of white light.

He was the Seventh Toa!

He could feel his body transforming as the mask's power flooded through him. He became taller, stronger, brighter. Light emanated from him, freezing the Fear-Rahkshi in its tracks.

The other six Toa gazed up at him in awe. They fell to their knees.

"Hail, brother Toa!" they said in one voice.

Takua stared at his own hand, which glowed white-hot with light energy. He picked up Jaller's kolhii stick, and a small spark jumped from his hand to the stick, transforming it into the Kolhii Staff of Light.

He turned to face the other Toa, his eyes

filled with awe and power. "I am Takanuva," he declared. "Toa of Light!"

As the white light bursting from him illuminated the entire temple, he bent and picked up Jaller's body. He carried it down the steps past the other Toa. Each of them raised his or her weapon in salute, then followed the Toa of Light with their heads solemnly bowed.

The next morning, Takanuva stood gazing down at the suva-style grave dome that had been raised in a quiet spot overlooking the Kini-Nui temple. A memorial pillar rose from the top of the dome, and Jaller's mask rested upon it.

Turaga Vakama stepped toward the Toa of Light. "You have finally found your own story," he said quietly, "and still you seek answers."

Takanuva stared at Jaller's mask. "All this, just to discover who I am?"

Vakama shrugged. "Mata Nui is wiser than all," he replied. "The path you walked was not to be here . . ." He paused and gestured at the temple. "But *here*." He tapped Takanuva on the chest. "You understand you have but one destiny."

Lewa helped Tahu attach a pipe to the vehicle they were building. "How will this wayfind the Makuta?" he asked.

Takanuva stepped forward, holding the six kraata in his fist. "What is the Makuta's shall return to him." He inserted the kraata into the slot they'd created for that purpose. They writhed angrily in their restraints.

Tahu looked up at the vehicle, which they were calling an Ussanui. They had created it out of parts of the defeated Rahkshi. Would it work?

Before long, all seven Toa were gathered around the completed Ussanui vehicle. Hahli walked up to them, carefully carrying Jaller's mask.

"Jaller was your Herald," she told Takanuva solemnly. "Let him continue to lead you to victory."

She stepped to the front of the vehicle, attaching the mask to it. Takanuva nodded.

"Well said, Hahli," he told her.

Pohatu cocked his head at the vehicle curiously. "Not much room in this transport," he said. "Where will we all sit, brother?"

Takanuva shook his head. "You won't," he replied. "You shall not join me."

The other Toa reacted with surprise. "But united, our power defeated the Rahkshi!" Pohatu reminded him.

Tahu nodded. "Certainly it will take nothing less to defeat Makuta!"

Takanuva turned away from them, staring at the transport. "I have but one destiny," he said. "Yours lie with the Matoran and the Turaga. Gather them and wait for my return."

He stepped forward, climbing into the Ussanui vehicle. At last, he turned to look at the Toa gathered below.

"Farewell," he told them.

The Ussanui rocketed through the tunnels beneath the Kini-Nui. Takanuva held on grimly, not thinking or moving. Just waiting.

Finally the Ussanui rounded another corner. An immense door blocked the tunnel, but the vehicle never slowed. It crashed straight into the door, cracking it open before bouncing off, skidding to a halt at last.

Takanuva opened his eyes. As he climbed out of the wrecked vehicle, there was a rattling sound behind him.

His eyes widened in amazement as a piece of the damaged vehicle was tossed aside and a familiar figure climbed out from the wreckage.

"Hahli!" Takanuva cried.

Hahli walked to the front of the vehicle and removed Jaller's mask. "Let *me* be your Chronicler," she told Takanuva with determination in her voice.

Takanuva hesitated, then nodded. Reaching into the wreckage long enough to pull out the six kraata, he turned and stepped through the cracked door into the dark chamber beyond.

A REAL HERO

Takanuva held the kraata tightly in his fist as he looked around the chamber. Behind him, Hahli started to step through the door, but he stopped her with a gesture. She backed off, watching through the crack.

By the light emanating from his own mask Takanuva could see several massive, carved stone columns holding up the stone ceiling.

Takanuva opened his hand. The kraata slithered free, writhing their way across the floor and around the pools, heading toward a dark doorway on the opposite end of the chamber. Two large red eyes opened in the darkness, staring toward the Toa.

"You can no longer hide in shadow," Takanuva said, his eyes tightening in resolve.

"I *am* shadow," Makuta's sinister voice rang out from the darkness. "The shadow that guards the gate. Now run along, or accept your doom."

Takanuva stepped forward boldly. Suddenly he realized what he needed to do. "I am done running. Mata Nui will be awoken this day." He turned to Hahli, still peering through the doorway behind him. "Hahli, summon the Matoran."

Hahli's face registered her shock at the request. But she nodded and hurried off.

Takanuva waited calmly as Makuta started to move out of the shadows. "Toa of Light," the dark one hissed. "Now so bold. But at heart, you are still just Takua."

He stepped into the light. The Mask of Shadow on his face glared down at Takanuva. Makuta was nearly twice the Toa's height.

"Are you truly prepared to face me?"

Though he tried to hide it, Takanuva was shocked at Makuta's size. But he held his ground as Makuta approached him.

"You failed to save your friend," Makuta

said. "You didn't even warn him. Perhaps for your next great failure . . ." He paused, holding out his arm. A Kolhii Staff of Shadow grew out of it. Then he motioned toward the doorway behind him. "A simple game of kolhii? Win and you may try to open the gate. When you lose, I'll have that mask."

"I will not lose!" Takanuva retorted, clutching his own staff tightly.

Makuta nodded, accepting the challenge. The surface of the nearest mercury pool rippled. A silvery ball slowly rose out of it, hovering in midair between Makuta and Takanuva.

Both players leaped toward the ball. Takanuva was faster and reached it first, snatching it in the scoop on one end of his kolhii staff. Dodging Makuta's swiping blow, he darted past him.

He landed on a perch along one of the pillars. Makuta followed, perching on another pillar. The ball of mercury in Takanuva's scoop transformed suddenly into a glowing ball of light. Takanuva launched it toward Makuta.

Makuta dodged the ball of light, which exploded against the pillar behind him.

Another ball of mercury rose out of the pool. This time Makuta was the faster one. He grabbed the ball with his kolhii staff, and it immediately transformed into a ball of dark shadow energy. He flung it at Takanuva.

The Toa leaped to the side. The ball of shadow crashed against another pillar, splintering it.

The kolhii match continued. Neither player spoke; neither hesitated. And neither managed to score a hit on the other. Every time a ball crashed out of the game, another rose from the mercury to take its place.

Finally Makuta launched a ball of darkness that flew toward Takanuva faster than ever. The Toa dodged it just in time, but the ball smashed into the pillar behind him with full force. The impact was too much for the structure — it splintered and came loose from the ceiling, plummeting into a hole that suddenly yawned open in the floor below it.

Takanuva managed to leap to safety, rolling to a stop inches from a pool of mercury. Makuta jumped down and swooped on the next ball of mercury before the Toa could react. Then he stalked toward Takanuva.

He laughed with dark triumph. "You know I cannot be beaten!"

With that, he launched the ball of shadow straight at Takanuva.

Hahli ran through the tunnels as fast as she could, still clutching Jaller's mask. The thought of her fallen friend gave strength to her legs and courage to her heart. Ahead of her, finally she saw a pinprick of daylight.

A moment later she burst out of the crater of the ruined suva dome into the main temple area at Kini-Nui. The six Turaga and the six Toa stood around the dome crater, waiting. The entire population of the island was gathered behind them on the hillsides surrounding the temple, waiting to hear the fate of the Toa of Light.

"I bring word from Takanuva!" Hahli blurted.

She climbed out of the hole, breathing hard. "He wants us to follow. We are to awaken Mata Nui today!"

The crowd, hearing the news, murmured uncertainly.

"A light among the shadows," Turaga Vakama said in a faraway voice. "The prophecy is fulfilled. We must go!"

Turaga Onewa's face was grim. "If we descend into those tunnels, we will never again return!"

The crowd's murmurs grew louder. The villagers looked by turns nervous, excited, and uncertain.

Hahli climbed up onto a chunk of stone and held up Jaller's mask. "This island is a great and wondrous place," she declared. "Never has any people been as blessed as we are to live in such a paradise."

All around her, Turaga and Matoran nodded in agreement. Taking strength from her own convictions — and her memories of Jaller — Hahli continued.

"I love my home," she said. "And Jaller loved it, too. But above all Jaller respected his duty. Let us repay him by doing *our* duty. Let us remember him by fulfilling our destiny! Let us go forward together." She glanced around at the crowd, which was hanging on her every word. "Let us awaken the Great Spirit!"

The crowd burst into loud cheers. Hahli sighed with relief. She had done her duty. Now it was time for the island's people to do theirs.

Takanuva barely managed to escape the ball of shadow. The effort of dodging it sent him flying off a pillar into space. He adjusted in midair, swinging his feet around until he was running straight down the pillar. The momentum carried him over to the mercury pool just as another ball rose from it.

He grabbed it in his kolhii net. As soon as it transformed into a ball of light, he turned and hurled it toward Makuta.

But the dark one was ready. He swung his own kolhii stick, catching the ball of light in his net and transforming it into darkness.

Takanuva gasped in shock. Then he leaped to the side as the ball came hurtling back toward him, shattering another pillar and sending it collapsing into the floor. Once again, the Toa of Light barely dodged in time, jumping over to another pillar — one of only two left standing in the cavern. He was growing tired. How much longer could he continue this game?

Makuta grabbed the next mercury ball and transformed it. Then he walked toward the two pillars, searching for his quarry.

"An audience gathers for your final failure, Toa of Light," Makuta said.

Takanuva leaped high up the pillar, staying just out of his opponent's sight. "Maybe they will not see me win today," he said. "But the Matoran will go on, and someday *they* will triumph."

"You actually believe I would let them return?" Makuta said. "After all the trouble they have been?"

Just outside the cavern, Hahli rode Pewku toward the door, leading the six Toa, the six Turaga, and the Matoran crowd behind her. The

Toa gathered around the crack in the doorway, looking through into Makuta's cavern.

There was only one pillar left standing now. Takanuva clung to it, while Makuta stood at the base, a ball of darkness quivering in his net. The dark one turned, glancing toward the doorway.

"Now that I have them," he said with malicious satisfaction, "they will not leave."

With a sudden horror, Takanuva realized the truth — he had led his people into a trap!

"NO!" he cried.

Makuta launched the ball of darkness toward the voice overhead. Takanuva ducked it. The ball struck the pillar, which started to collapse.

Takanuva landed on the ground on one side of the mercury pool. Makuta stood on the other. Without hesitating, the Toa of Light flipped himself over the mercury toward his enemy.

A ball of mercury rose out of the pool, and Takanuva grabbed it in midflip, transforming it into a ball of light. He immediately rolled into his special kolhii move, somersaulting and throwing the ball at the same time.

This time it worked — the ball of light flew right into Makuta's chest!

The force of the impact knocked Makuta backward across the chamber. He staggered, then dropped to his knees with a mighty crash. Light energy flashed through his body.

Makuta roared in pain as the light energy weakened him. "Well played, Toa," he croaked.

Takanuva stepped forward. He had done it! He had finally defeated his enemy!

But Makuta wasn't quite finished yet. As the Toa approached, the dark one suddenly flung out his hand, shoving Takanuva backward with surprising force.

Takanuva grunted, startled. He fell back hard, landing near the pool of mercury.

Makuta climbed to his feet. "Now I will protect Mata Nui from you," he snarled, marching toward the Toa of Light.

"Protect him?" Confused, Takanuva lowered his staff.

"Sleep spares him pain!" Makuta said. "Awake, he suffers."

He continued stalking toward Takanuva, who found himself backing closer and closer to the pool of mercury. The Toa of Light wasn't sure what to think of the dark one's words. How could he think that Mata Nui was better off remaining asleep? How could he think that was best for the island?

"But he does not live," he protested, still perplexed.

Makuta raised his kolhii staff. Utter determination danced in his red eyes. "My duty remains to the shadows."

Suddenly Takanuva smiled. The light had dawned in his mind — he knew what he had to do.

"Then let's take a closer look at those shadows," he said.

He dropped his kolhii staff and leaped toward Makuta, landing on his chest so that the two of them were face-to-face. With one hand Takanuva grabbed the Mask of Shadow, yanking it off of Makuta's head. His other hand pulled his own mask free. Before Makuta could react, the Toa had switched the masks, shoving the Mask of Light onto the dark one's face and placing the Mask of Shadow over his own face.

"NO!" Makuta howled.

Makuta staggered in a circle, the mask pulsing on his face. Then he toppled backward into the mercury pool, pulling Takanuva along with him.

The other six Toa rushed into the room, followed by the Turaga and the others. They all gathered around the pool. The still, silvery surface remained unbroken for a long, long moment. The Toa exchanged glances, not sure what to think.

Suddenly arcs of dark and light energy shot out of the mercury and danced across the surface. The Matoran took a wary step back.

Then a huge head rose from the steaming mercury. Makuta? No, it wasn't the dark one — at least not completely. It was the merged face of Takanuva and Makuta — half Mask of Light, half Mask of Shadow. An enormous merged figure continued to rise slowly out of the pool, half light and half shadow.

Takutanuva.

The light side of the mask spoke. "Light has revealed the will of Mata Nui," Takanuva's voice said.

"Our brother must be awakened," the Makuta side added.

The Toa, Turaga, and Matoran glanced at one another. None of them knew what to do or think now.

Takutanuva stepped out of the pool and walked toward the huge door set into the wall on the far side of the cavern. He crouched down, his fingers gouging the metal of the door as he tried to lift it. The door creaked and groaned, then slowly began to rise.

As Takutanuva struggled under the weight of the giant door, the Toa and the others stepped forward uncertainly and walked through into the chamber beyond. Hahli was still carrying Jaller's mask as she stepped past the giant two-sided figure.

"Hold, little one," Makuta's voice stopped her. "That mask needs life."

The shadowy side of Takutanuva reached out a hand. A powerful pulse of dark and light energy shot out from his fingertip, blasting into Jaller's mask.

Hahli stepped back as the mask took on a life of its own. As she watched in amazement, Jaller's body quickly regenerated from the mask — his head, his body, his legs bursting into existence out of nothing. A dim glow lit up the eyes behind the mask, and a moment later Jaller fell backward weakly.

Hahli caught him, stunned by what she had just seen. Could it really be? Could her friend have been brought back?

"Jaller!" she cried.

Jaller merely groaned in response, trying to take in what was happening.

But the energy of re-creating the brave Matoran had taken too much out of Takutanuva. He strained against the weight of the door, but it was no use. The metal door smashed down on him, sending up a thick cloud of dust that obscured the onlookers' view.

The Toa and Matoran bowed their heads sadly. Jaller stepped forward, heartbroken.

"Takua!" he cried as Pewku whined sorrowfully nearby.

The cloud of dust swirled vigorously. Suddenly, a figure stepped out of it — Takanuva!

As Hahli gasped in surprise, Jaller raced toward his friend. Pewku ran even faster, leaping onto Takanuva with joyful cries.

"You're alive!" Jaller exclaimed gleefully, hardly seeming to notice his friend's new form. Then he frowned. "Kolhii-head! You could've been Makuta bones!"

Takanuva grinned. "Could've been, but I'm not."

Turaga Vakama raised his staff, interrupting the friends' moment. "Let us awaken the Great Spirit."

Hahli, Jaller, and Takanuva followed the Turaga to the far end of the new chamber. There, a ledge plunged away into dark nothingness.

"Unity!" Turaga Vakama said solemnly. "Duty! Destiny!"

As he spoke, Takanuva's power illuminated his companions and himself. Their light shone down into the abyss, revealing what lay below.

The Matoran gasped in amazement as they saw a strange new world stretching out below them. The chamber at the bottom of the cliff was indescribably huge — it stretched farther than the eye could see. Strange structures dotted the landscape, and flashes of energy danced here and there.

Takanuva nodded as he surveyed. *This is it,* he thought as a feeling of certainty settled through him. *Soon we will understand everything. Who we are. Where we come from. Who sent us.*

Our destiny.